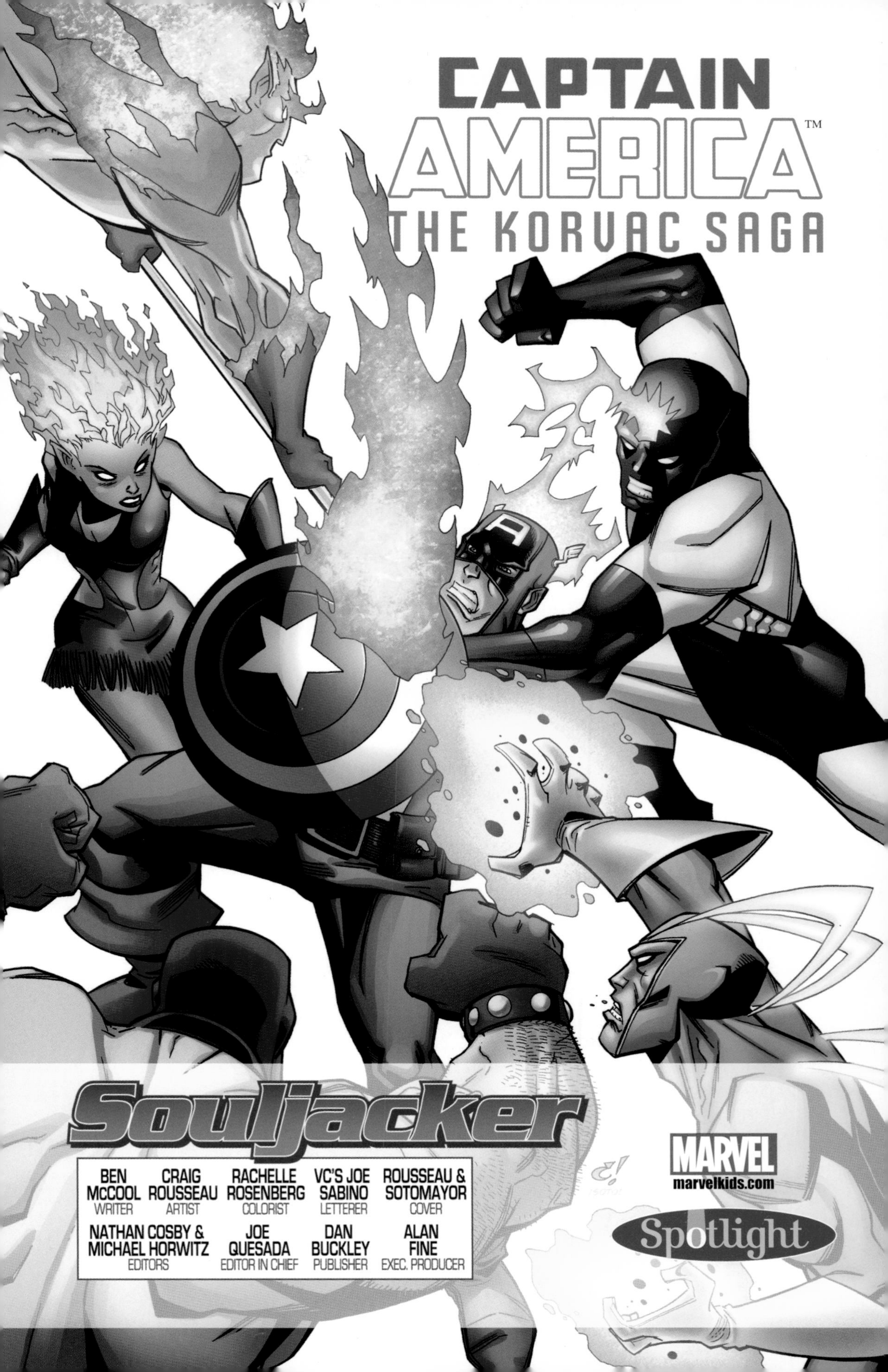
CAPTAIN AMERICA™
THE KORVAC SAGA
Souljacker
BEN McCOOL WRITER
CRAIG ROUSSEAU ARTIST
RACHELLE ROSENBERG COLORIST
VC'S JOE SABINO LETTERER
ROUSSEAU & SOTOMAYOR COVER
NATHAN COSBY & MICHAEL HORWITZ EDITORS
JOE QUESADA EDITOR IN CHIEF
DAN BUCKLEY PUBLISHER
ALAN FINE EXEC. PRODUCER
MARVEL
marvelkids.com
Spotlight

visit us at www.abdopublishing.com

Reinforced library bound edition published in 2013 by Spotlight, a division of the ABDO Group, PO Box 398166, Minneapolis, MN 55439. Spotlight produces high-quality reinforced library bound editions for schools and libraries. Published by agreement with Marvel Entertainment, LLC. The stories, characters, and incidents mentioned are entirely fictional. All rights reserved. Used under authorization.

Printed in the United States of America, North Mankato, Minnesota.
052012
092012
♻ This book contains at least 10% recycled materials.

marvelkids.com

TM & © 2012 Marvel & Subs.

Library of Congress Cataloging-in-Publication Data

McCool, Ben.
  Captain America : the Korvac saga / story by Ben McCool ; art by Craig Rousseau. -- Reinforced library bound ed.
     <v. 1-> cm.
  "Marvel."
  Summary: Captain America, a proud member of the Avengers, is still trying to find his way in a strange new world when he discovers his connection to a mysterious man named Korvac, who claims to be similarly displaced in time.
  Contents: [v. 1]. Strange days --
  ISBN 978-1-61479-019-8 (Strange days: #1 : alk. paper) -- ISBN 978-1-61479-020-4 (Souljacker: #2 : alk. paper) -- ISBN 978-1-61479-021-1 (The traveler: #3 : alk. paper) -- ISBN 978-1-61479-022-8 (The star lord: #4 : alk. paper)
  1. Graphic novels. [1. Graphic novels. 2. Superheroes--Fiction. 3. Space and time--Fiction.] I. Rousseau, Craig, ill. II. Title.
  PZ7.7.M415Cap 2012
  741.5'973--dc23
                              2012000931

ISBN 978-1-61479-020-4 (reinforced library edition)

All Spotlight books are reinforced library binding
and manufactured in the United States of America.

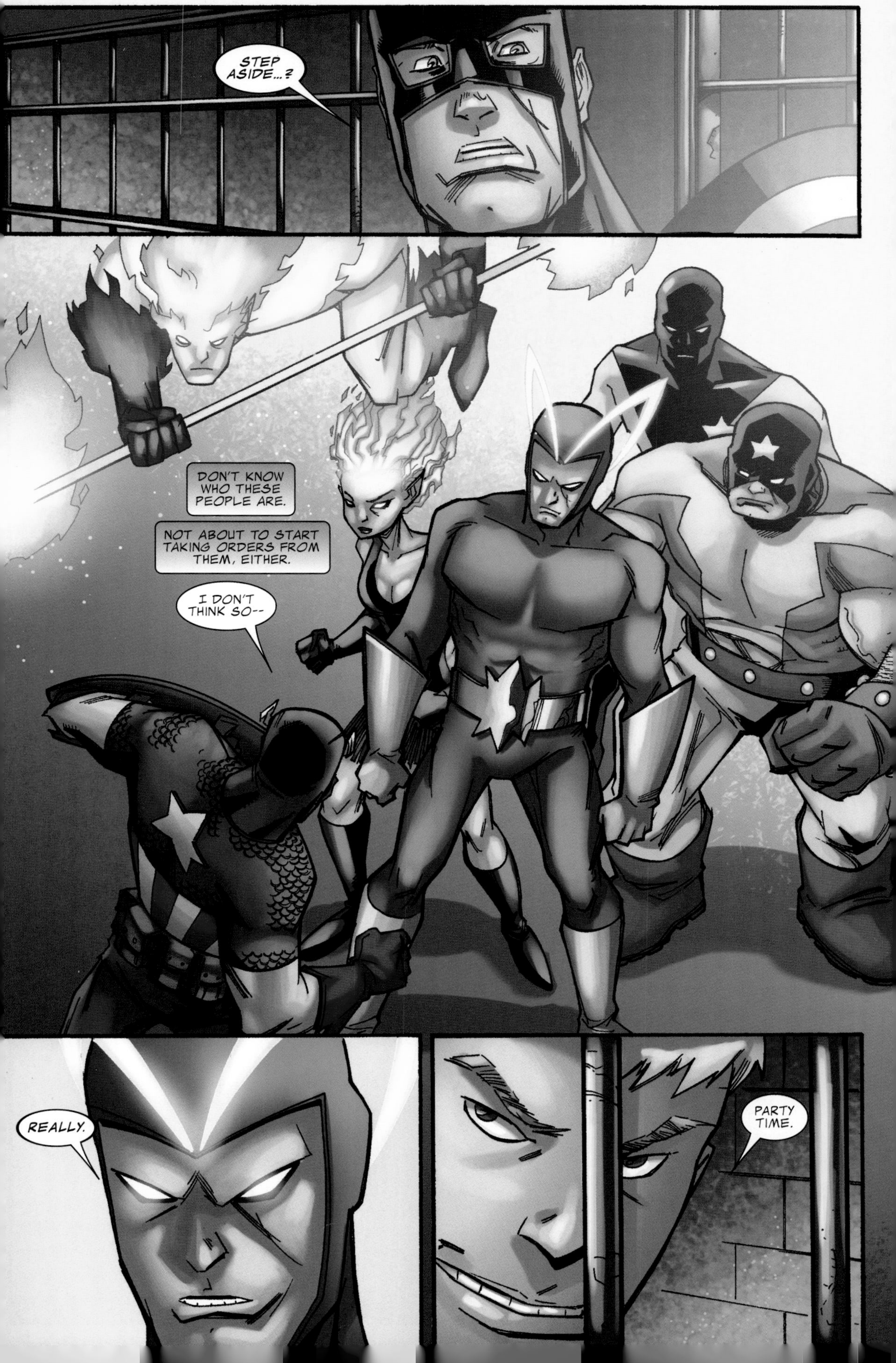
STEP ASIDE...?
DON'T KNOW WHO THESE PEOPLE ARE.
NOT ABOUT TO START TAKING ORDERS FROM THEM, EITHER.
I DON'T THINK SO--
REALLY.
PARTY TIME.

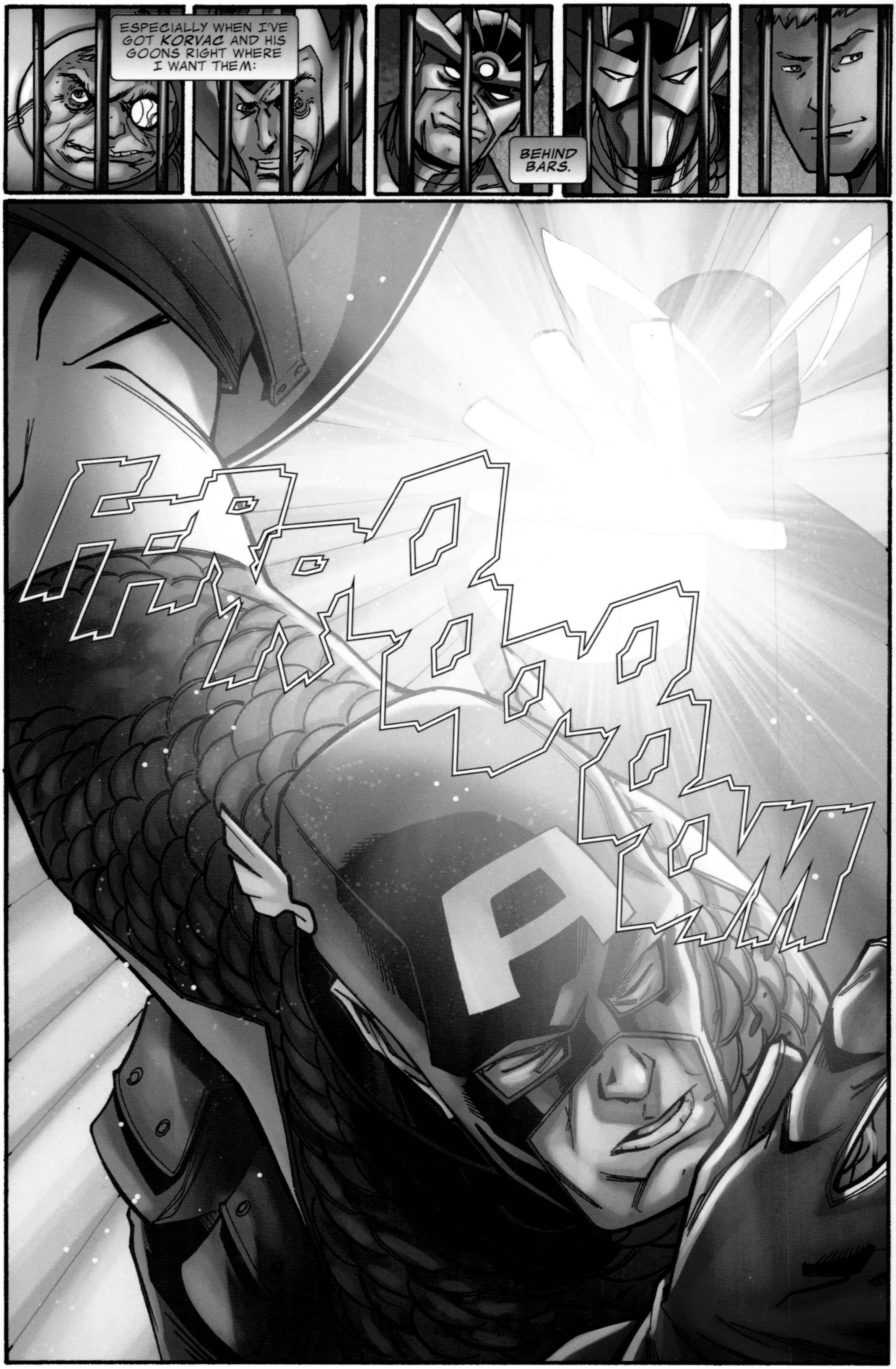
ESPECIALLY WHEN I'VE GOT KORVAC AND HIS GOONS RIGHT WHERE I WANT THEM:
BEHIND BARS.

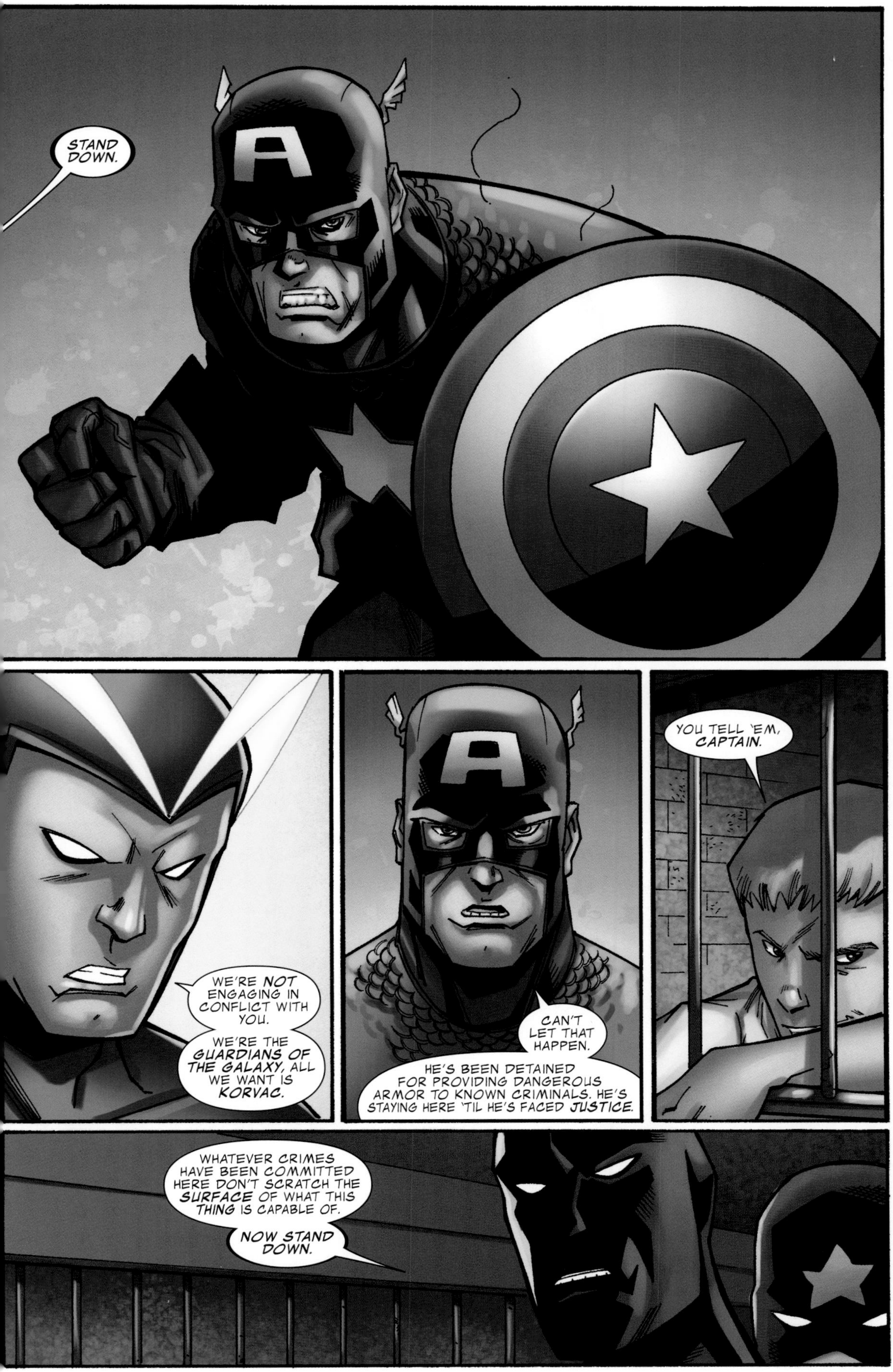
STAND DOWN.
WE'RE NOT ENGAGING IN CONFLICT WITH YOU.
WE'RE THE GUARDIANS OF THE GALAXY, ALL WE WANT IS KORVAC.
CAN'T LET THAT HAPPEN.
HE'S BEEN DETAINED FOR PROVIDING DANGEROUS ARMOR TO KNOWN CRIMINALS. HE'S STAYING HERE 'TIL HE'S FACED JUSTICE.
YOU TELL 'EM, CAPTAIN.
WHATEVER CRIMES HAVE BEEN COMMITTED HERE DON'T SCRATCH THE SURFACE OF WHAT THIS THING IS CAPABLE OF.
NOW STAND DOWN.

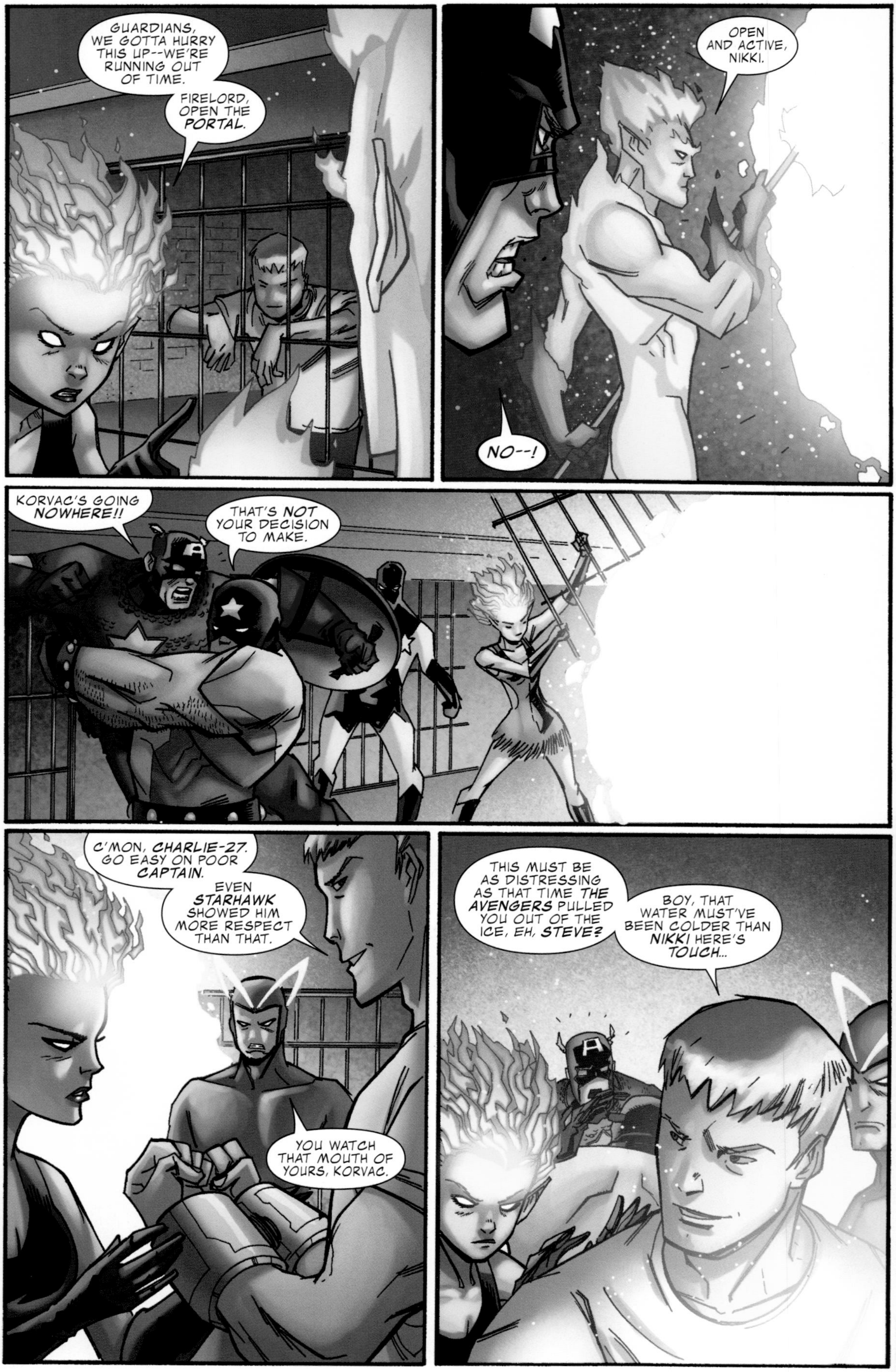
GUARDIANS, WE GOTTA HURRY THIS UP--WE'RE RUNNING OUT OF TIME.
FIRELORD, OPEN THE PORTAL.
OPEN AND ACTIVE, NIKKI.
NO--!
KORVAC'S GOING NOWHERE!!
THAT'S NOT YOUR DECISION TO MAKE.
C'MON, CHARLIE-27. GO EASY ON POOR CAPTAIN.
EVEN STARHAWK SHOWED HIM MORE RESPECT THAN THAT.
YOU WATCH THAT MOUTH OF YOURS, KORVAC.
THIS MUST BE AS DISTRESSING AS THAT TIME THE AVENGERS PULLED YOU OUT OF THE ICE, EH, STEVE?
BOY, THAT WATER MUST'VE BEEN COLDER THAN NIKKI HERE'S TOUCH...

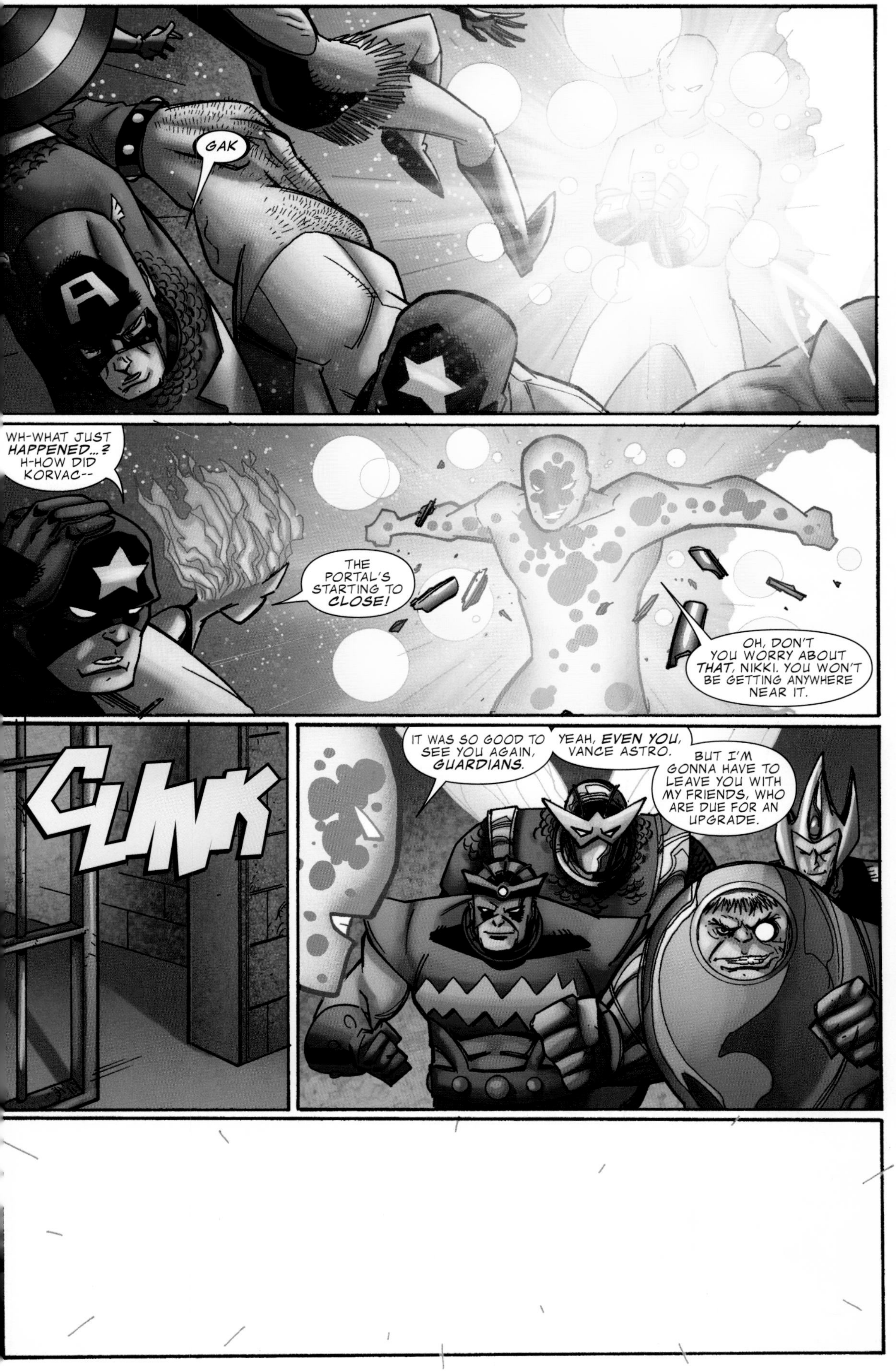
GAK
WH-WHAT JUST HAPPENED...? H-HOW DID KORVAC--
THE PORTAL'S STARTING TO CLOSE!
OH, DON'T YOU WORRY ABOUT THAT, NIKKI. YOU WON'T BE GETTING ANYWHERE NEAR IT.
CLINK
IT WAS SO GOOD TO SEE YOU AGAIN, GUARDIANS.
YEAH, EVEN YOU, VANCE ASTRO.
BUT I'M GONNA HAVE TO LEAVE YOU WITH MY FRIENDS, WHO ARE DUE FOR AN UPGRADE.

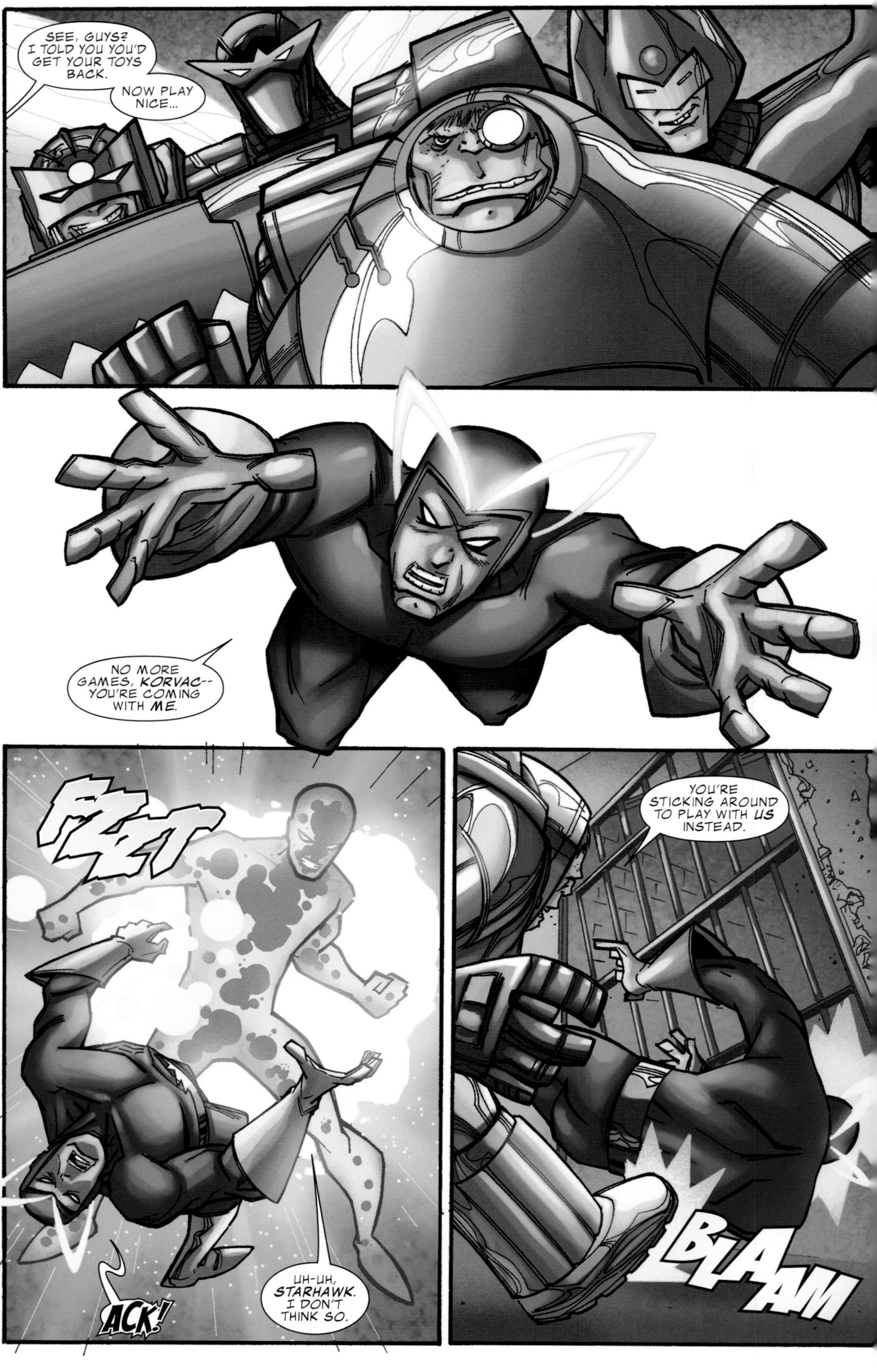
SEE, GUYS? I TOLD YOU YOU'D GET YOUR TOYS BACK.
NOW PLAY NICE...
NO MORE GAMES, KORVAC-- YOU'RE COMING WITH ME.
FZZT
UH-UH, STARHAWK. I DON'T THINK SO.
ACK!
YOU'RE STICKING AROUND TO PLAY WITH US INSTEAD.
BLAAM

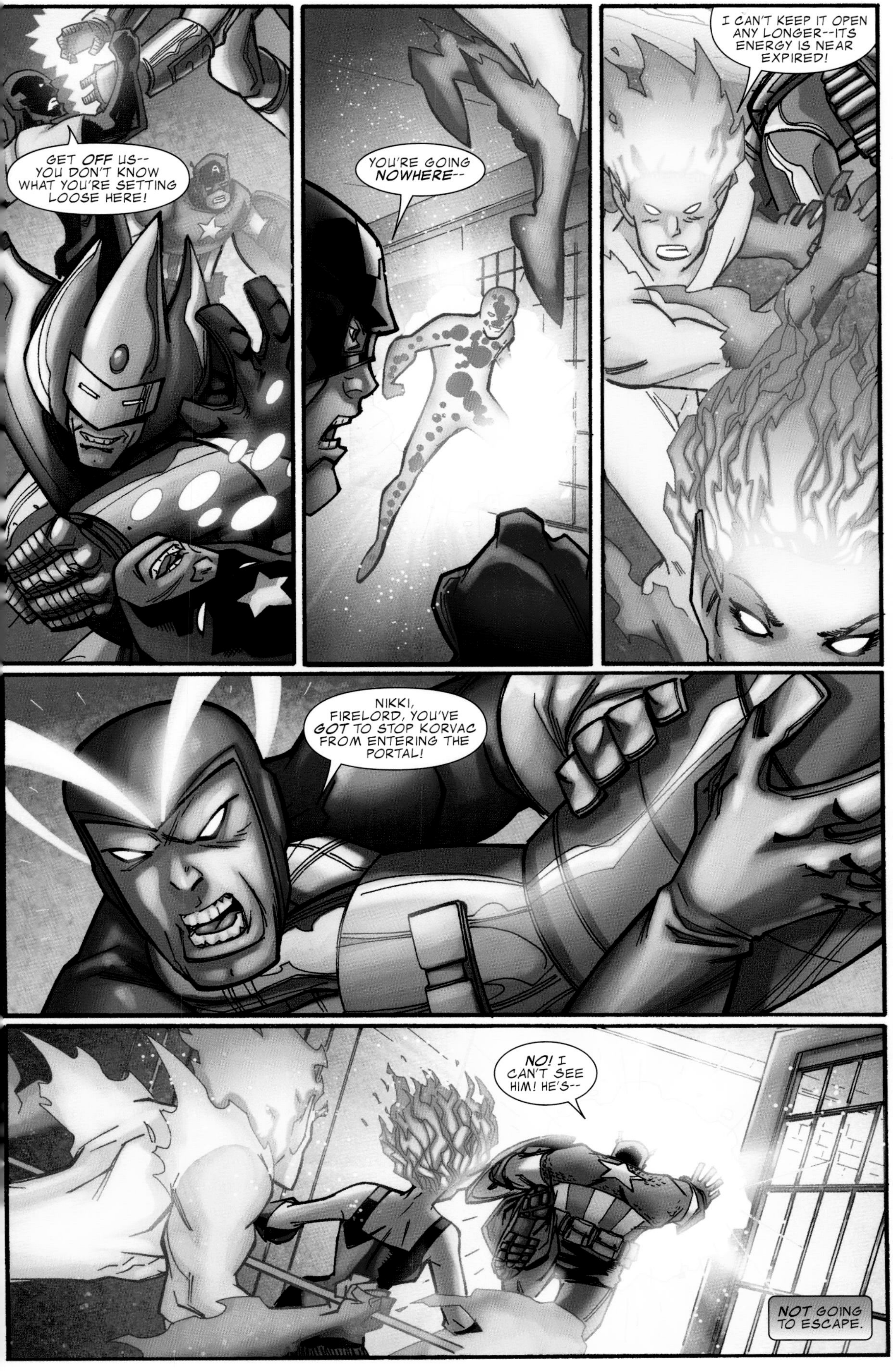
GET OFF US-- YOU DON'T KNOW WHAT YOU'RE SETTING LOOSE HERE!
YOU'RE GOING NOWHERE--
I CAN'T KEEP IT OPEN ANY LONGER--ITS ENERGY IS NEAR EXPIRED!
NIKKI, FIRELORD, YOU'VE GOT TO STOP KORVAC FROM ENTERING THE PORTAL!
NO! I CAN'T SEE HIM! HE'S--
NOT GOING TO ESCAPE.

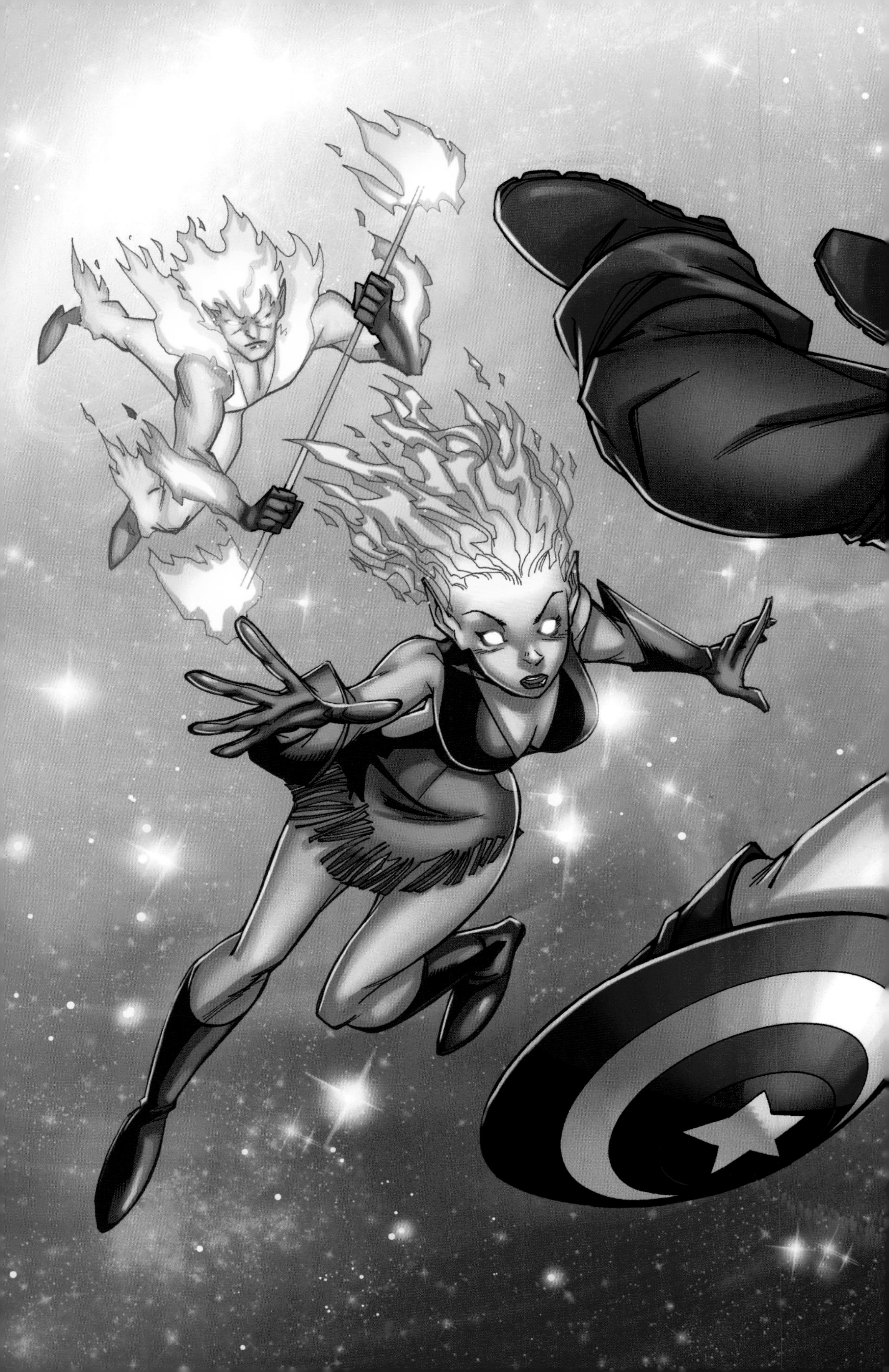

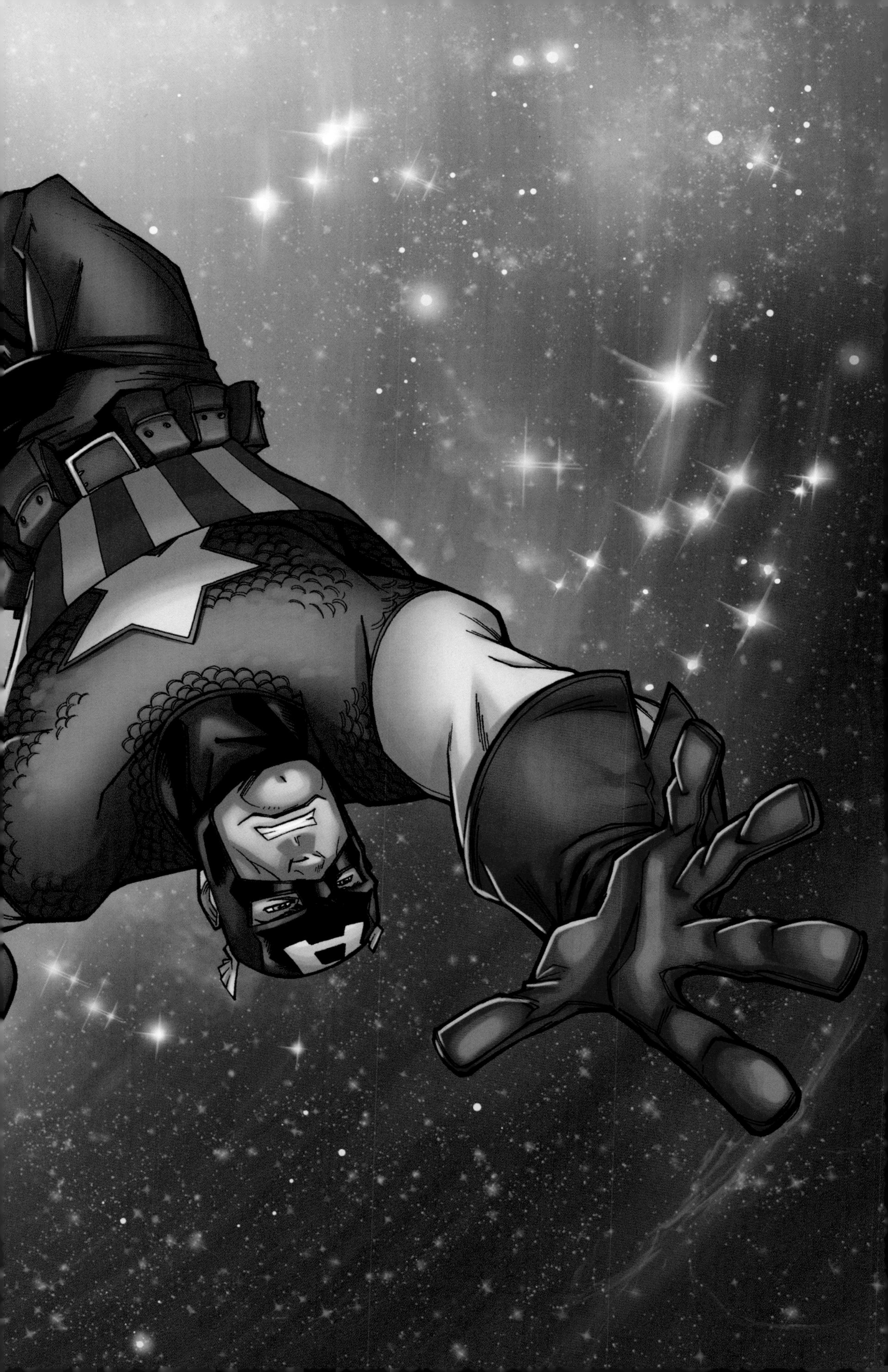

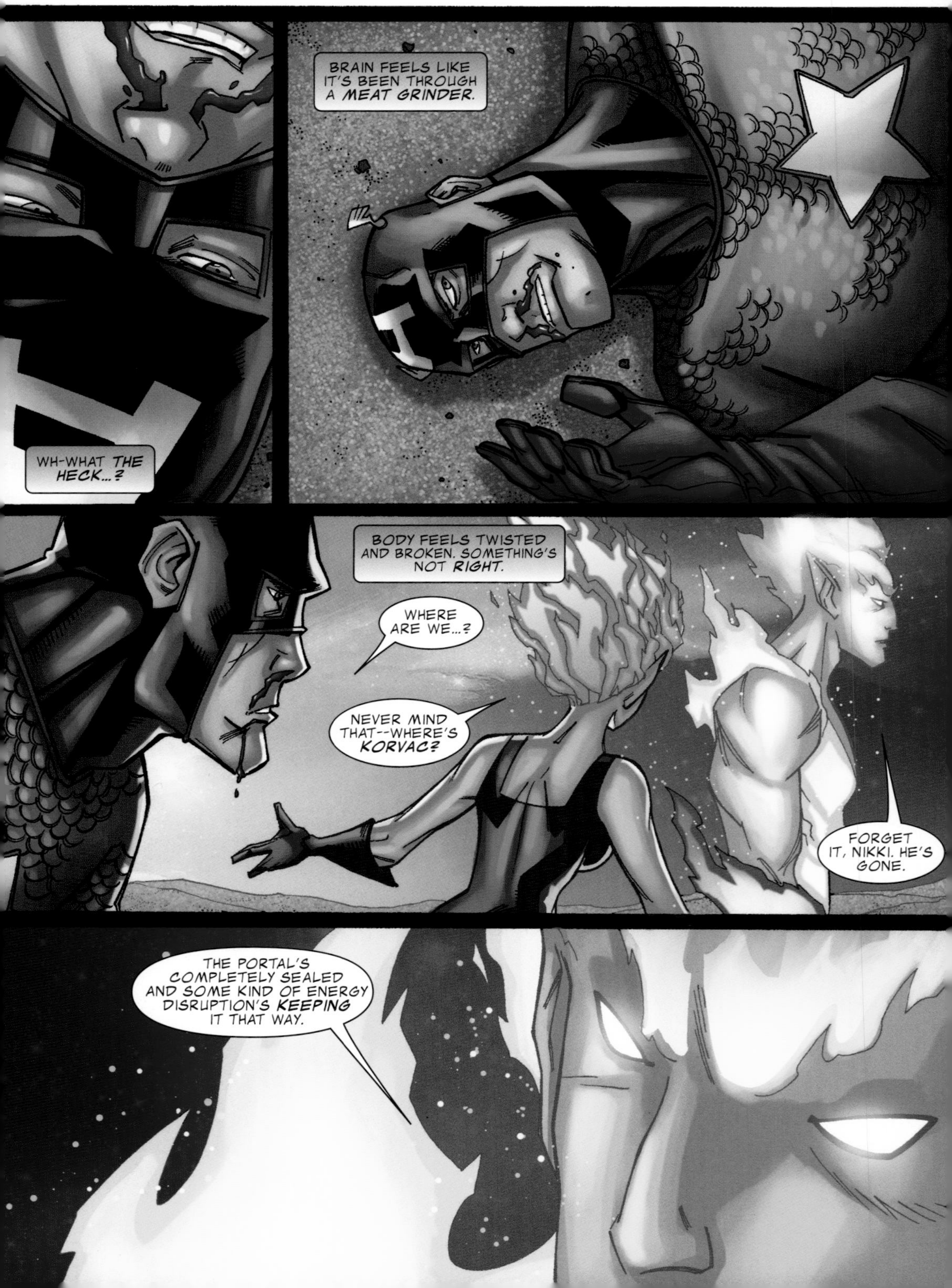
WH-WHAT THE HECK...?
BRAIN FEELS LIKE IT'S BEEN THROUGH A MEAT GRINDER.
BODY FEELS TWISTED AND BROKEN. SOMETHING'S NOT RIGHT.
WHERE ARE WE...?
NEVER MIND THAT--WHERE'S KORVAC?
FORGET IT, NIKKI. HE'S GONE.
THE PORTAL'S COMPLETELY SEALED AND SOME KIND OF ENERGY DISRUPTION'S KEEPING IT THAT WAY.

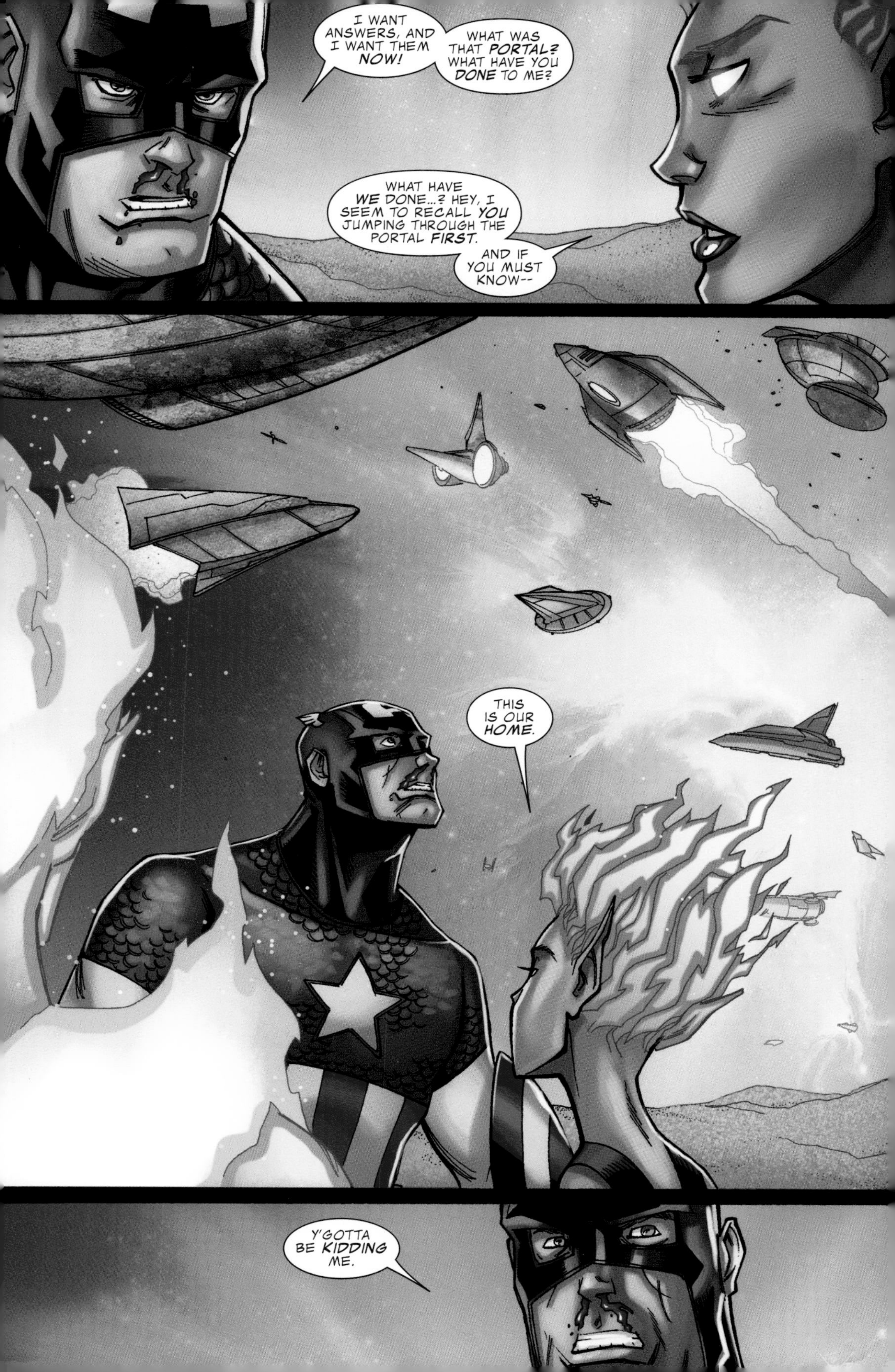
I WANT ANSWERS, AND I WANT THEM NOW!
WHAT WAS THAT PORTAL? WHAT HAVE YOU DONE TO ME?
WHAT HAVE WE DONE...? HEY, I SEEM TO RECALL YOU JUMPING THROUGH THE PORTAL FIRST.
AND IF YOU MUST KNOW--
THIS IS OUR HOME.
Y'GOTTA BE KIDDING ME.

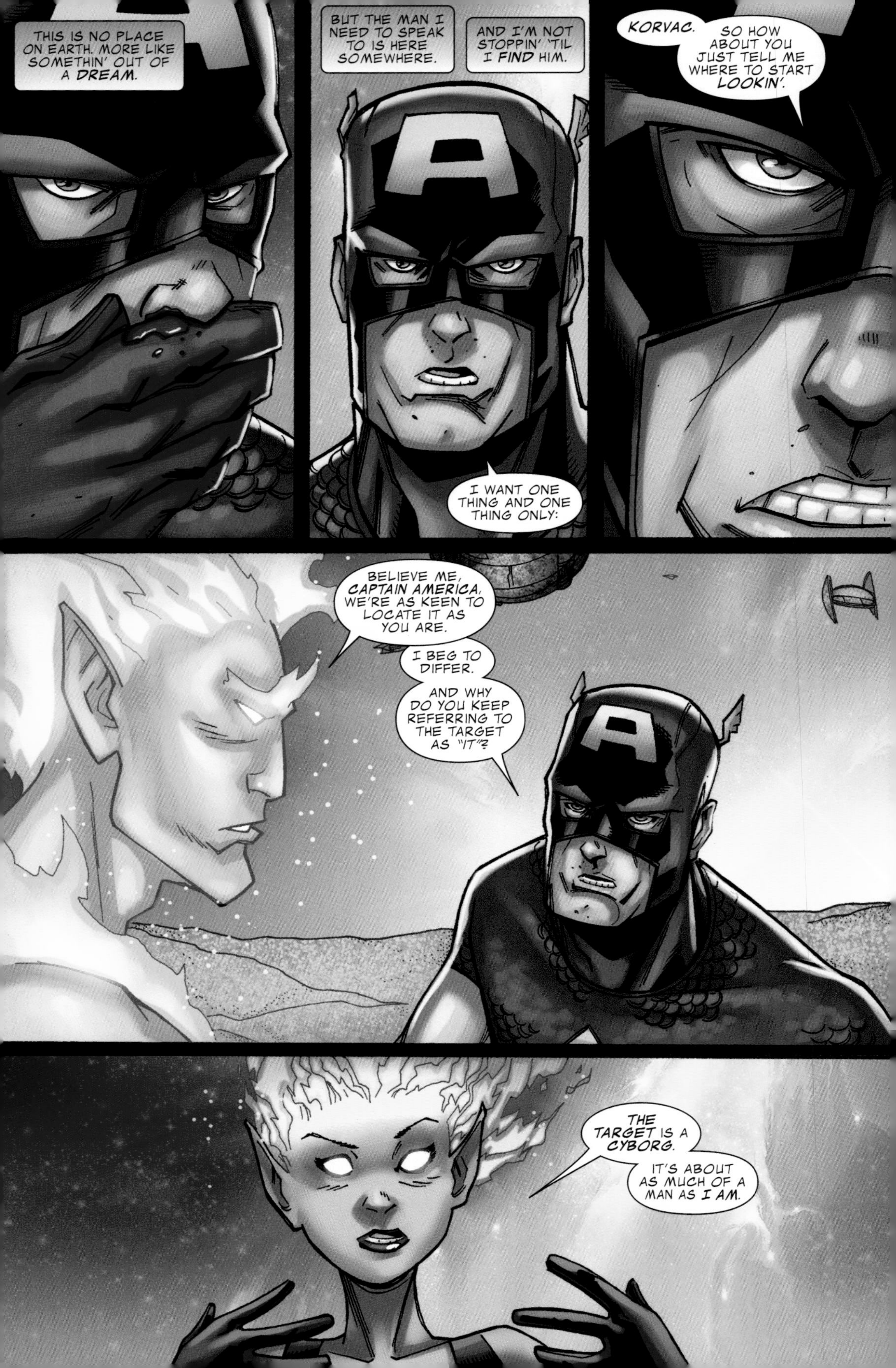
THIS IS NO PLACE ON EARTH. MORE LIKE SOMETHIN' OUT OF A DREAM.
BUT THE MAN I NEED TO SPEAK TO IS HERE SOMEWHERE.
AND I'M NOT STOPPIN' 'TIL I FIND HIM.
I WANT ONE THING AND ONE THING ONLY:
KORVAC.
SO HOW ABOUT YOU JUST TELL ME WHERE TO START LOOKIN'.
BELIEVE ME, CAPTAIN AMERICA, WE'RE AS KEEN TO LOCATE IT AS YOU ARE.
I BEG TO DIFFER.
AND WHY DO YOU KEEP REFERRING TO THE TARGET AS "IT"?
THE TARGET IS A CYBORG.
IT'S ABOUT AS MUCH OF A MAN AS I AM.

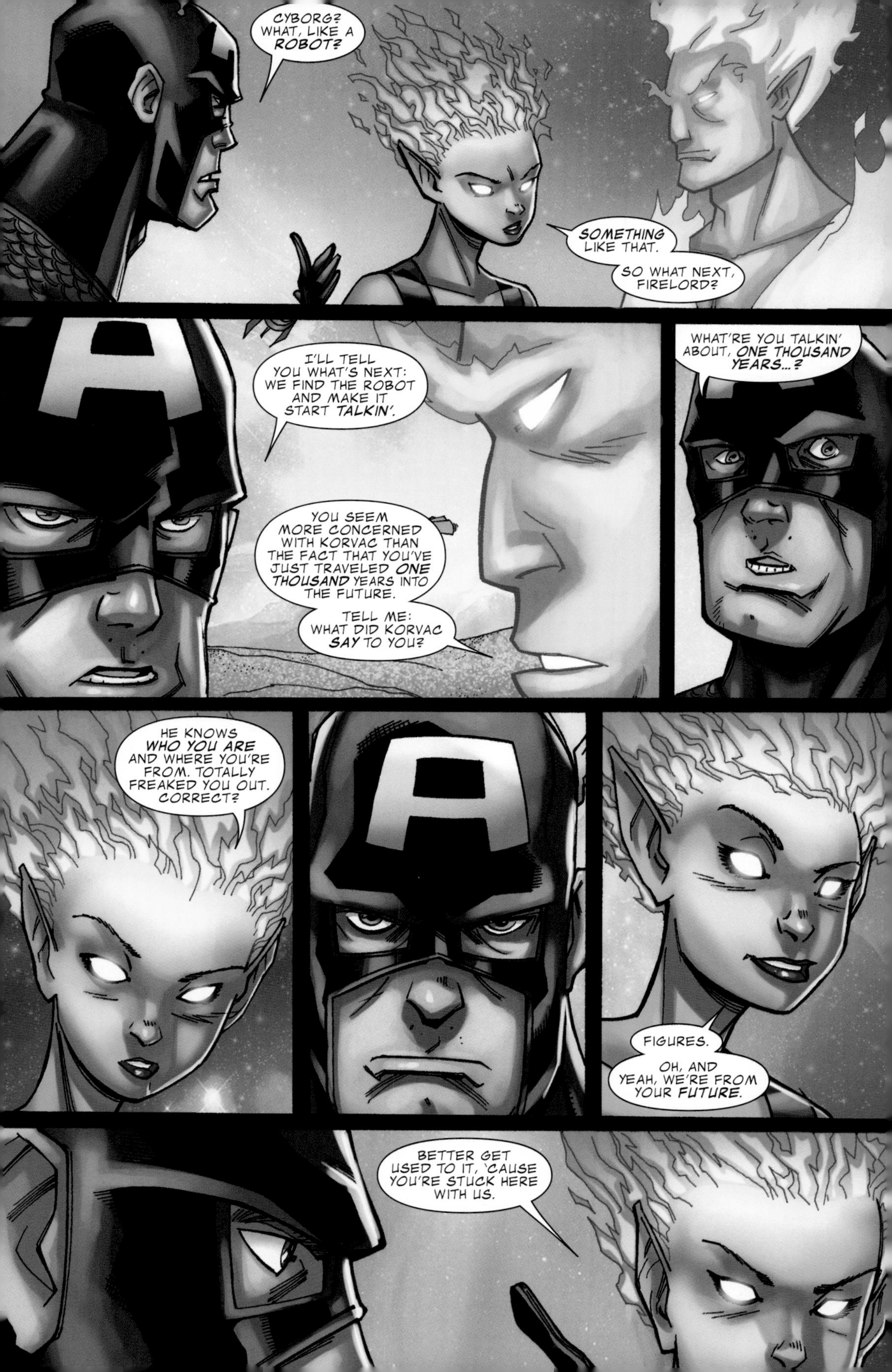
CYBORG? WHAT, LIKE A ROBOT?
SOMETHING LIKE THAT.
SO WHAT NEXT, FIRELORD?
I'LL TELL YOU WHAT'S NEXT: WE FIND THE ROBOT AND MAKE IT START TALKIN'.
YOU SEEM MORE CONCERNED WITH KORVAC THAN THE FACT THAT YOU'VE JUST TRAVELED ONE THOUSAND YEARS INTO THE FUTURE.
TELL ME: WHAT DID KORVAC SAY TO YOU?
WHAT'RE YOU TALKIN' ABOUT, ONE THOUSAND YEARS...?
HE KNOWS WHO YOU ARE AND WHERE YOU'RE FROM. TOTALLY FREAKED YOU OUT. CORRECT?
FIGURES.
OH, AND YEAH, WE'RE FROM YOUR FUTURE.
BETTER GET USED TO IT, 'CAUSE YOU'RE STUCK HERE WITH US.

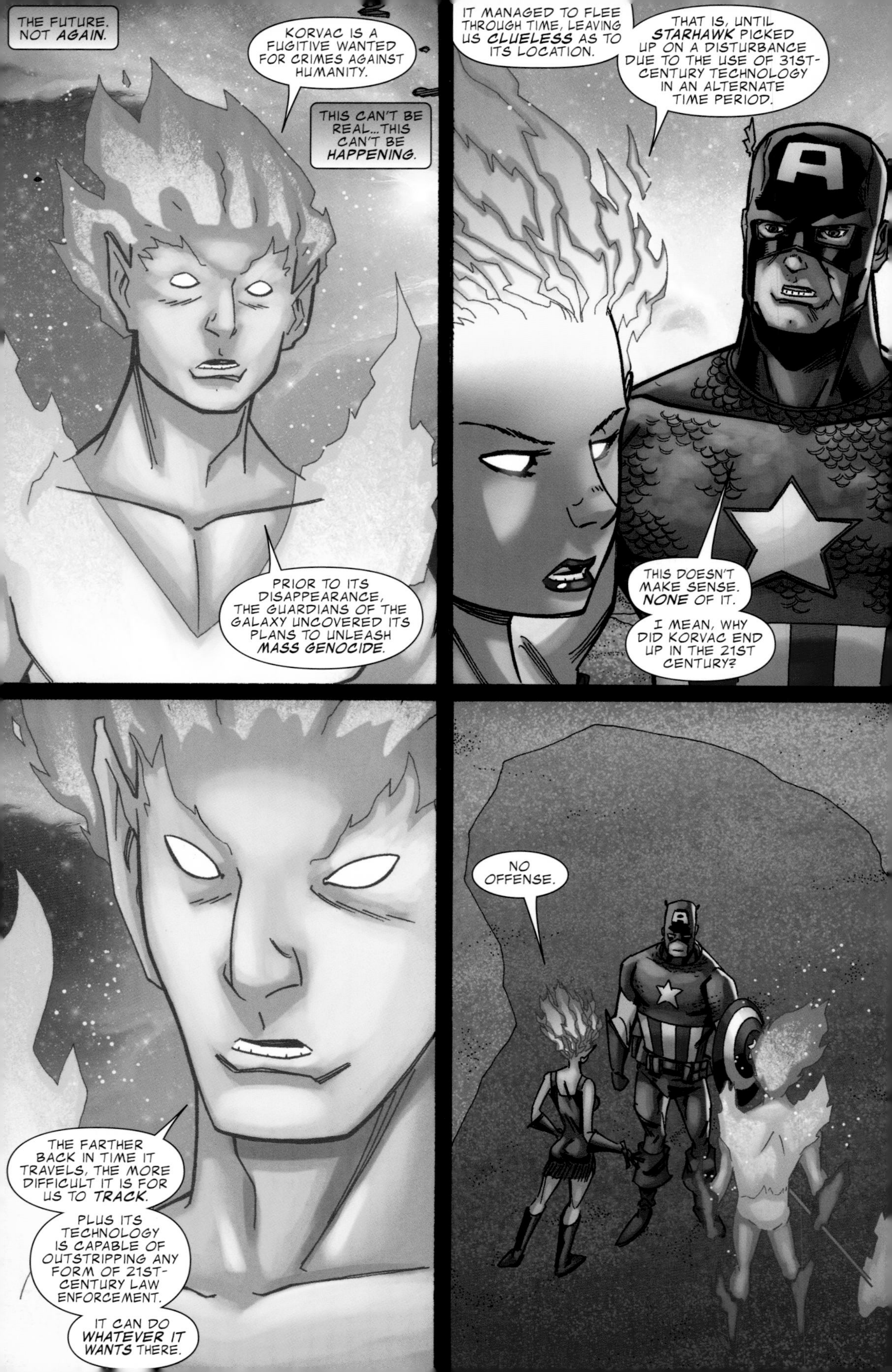
THE FUTURE. NOT AGAIN.
KORVAC IS A FUGITIVE WANTED FOR CRIMES AGAINST HUMANITY.
THIS CAN'T BE REAL...THIS CAN'T BE HAPPENING.
PRIOR TO ITS DISAPPEARANCE, THE GUARDIANS OF THE GALAXY UNCOVERED ITS PLANS TO UNLEASH MASS GENOCIDE.
IT MANAGED TO FLEE THROUGH TIME, LEAVING US CLUELESS AS TO ITS LOCATION.
THAT IS, UNTIL STARHAWK PICKED UP ON A DISTURBANCE DUE TO THE USE OF 31ST-CENTURY TECHNOLOGY IN AN ALTERNATE TIME PERIOD.
THIS DOESN'T MAKE SENSE. NONE OF IT.
I MEAN, WHY DID KORVAC END UP IN THE 21ST CENTURY?
THE FARTHER BACK IN TIME IT TRAVELS, THE MORE DIFFICULT IT IS FOR US TO TRACK.
PLUS ITS TECHNOLOGY IS CAPABLE OF OUTSTRIPPING ANY FORM OF 21ST-CENTURY LAW ENFORCEMENT.
IT CAN DO WHATEVER IT WANTS THERE.
NO OFFENSE.

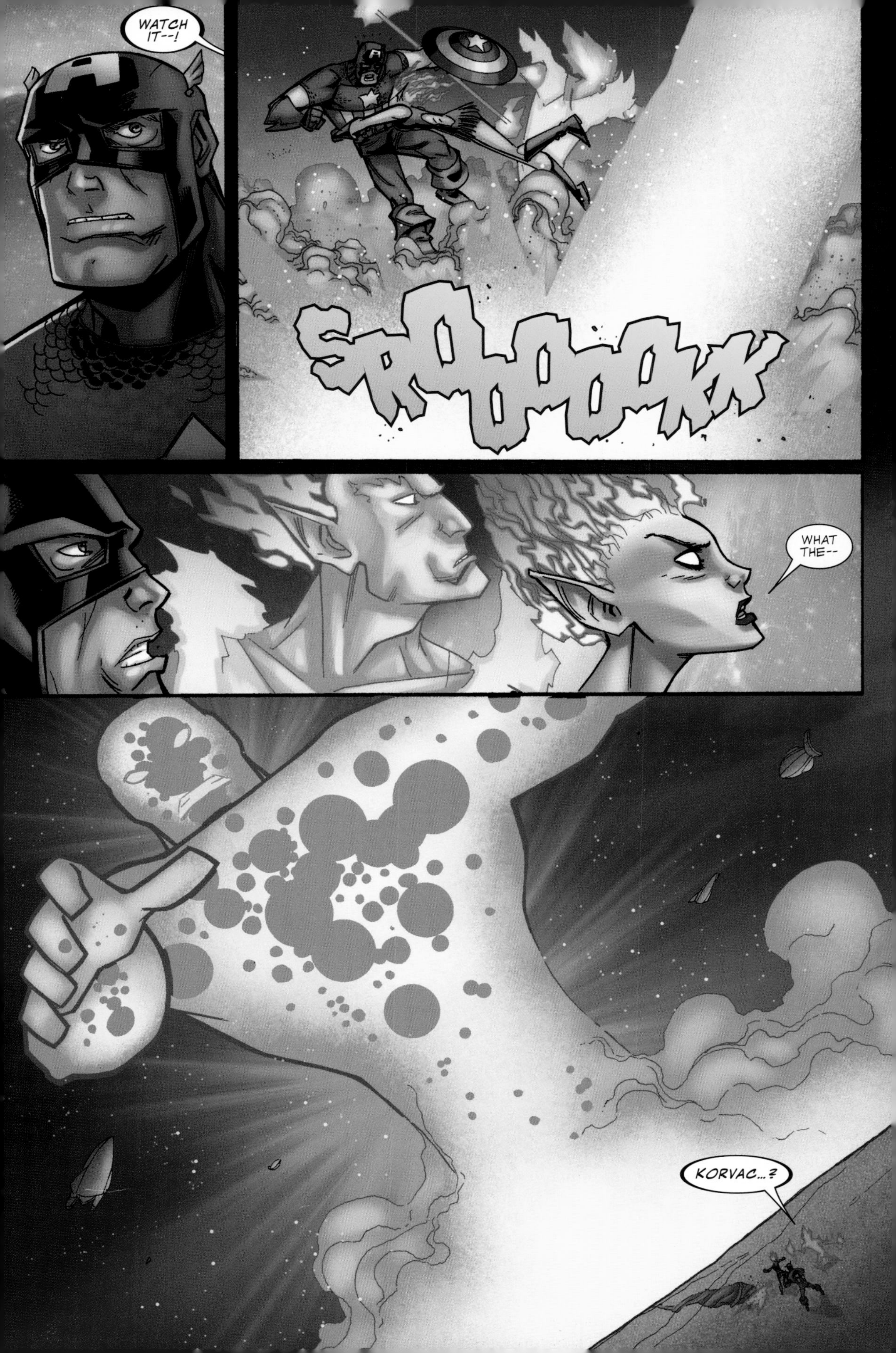
WATCH IT--!
SPROOOOKK
WHAT THE--
KORVAC...?

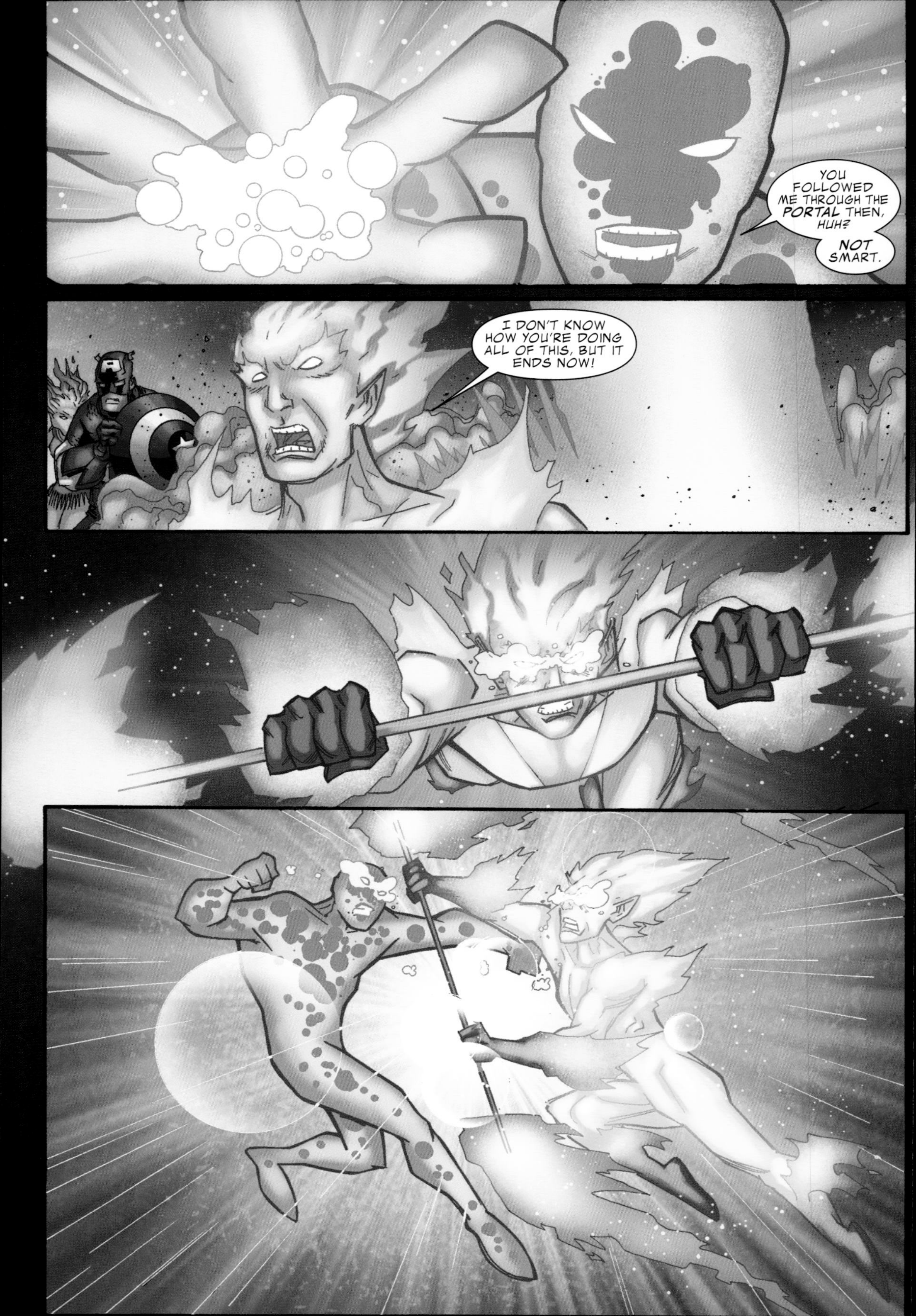
YOU FOLLOWED ME THROUGH THE PORTAL THEN, HUH?
NOT SMART.
I DON'T KNOW HOW YOU'RE DOING ALL OF THIS, BUT IT ENDS NOW!

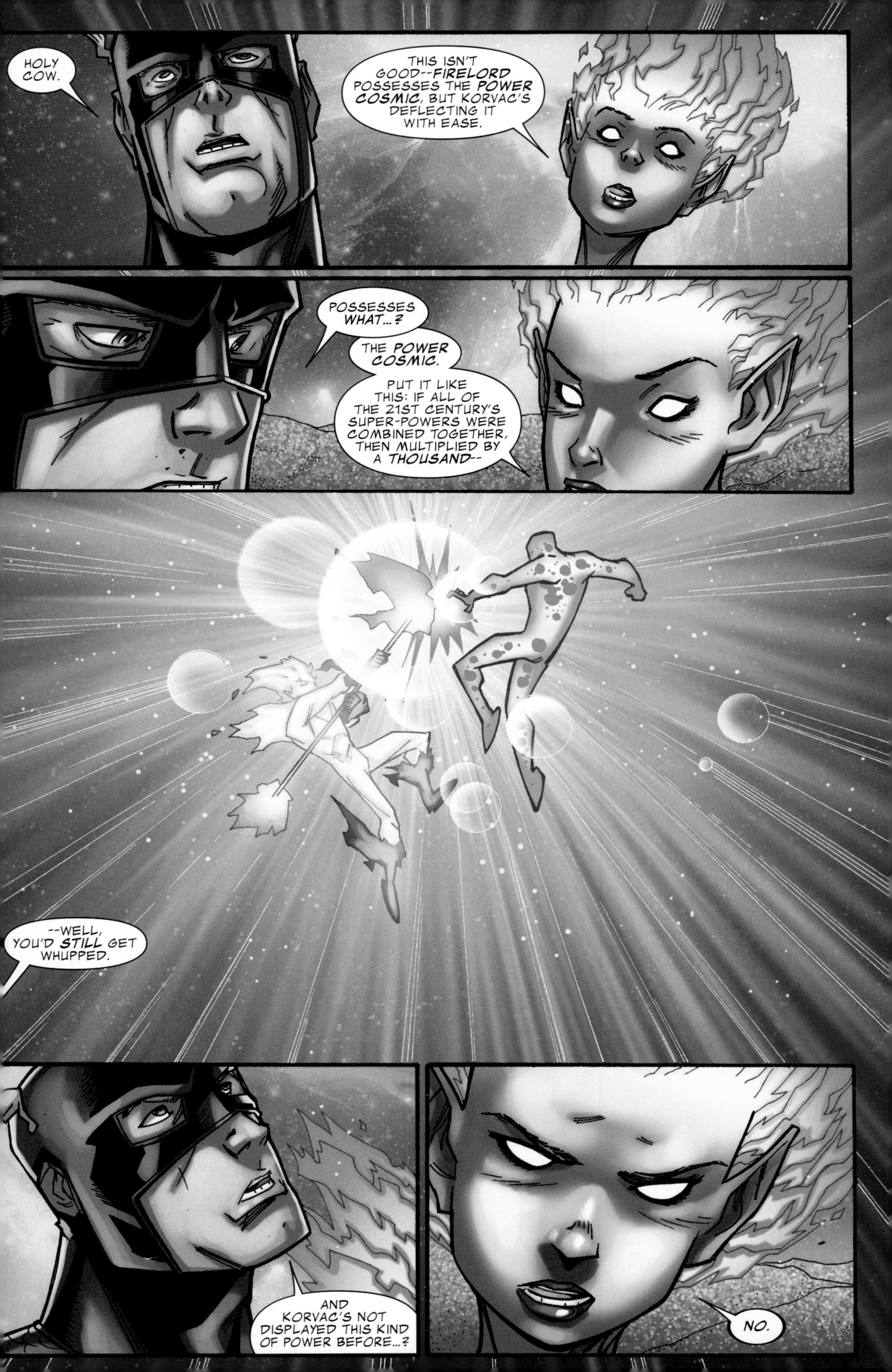
HOLY COW.
THIS ISN'T GOOD--FIRELORD POSSESSES THE POWER COSMIC, BUT KORVAC'S DEFLECTING IT WITH EASE.
POSSESSES WHAT...?
THE POWER COSMIC.
PUT IT LIKE THIS: IF ALL OF THE 21ST CENTURY'S SUPER-POWERS WERE COMBINED TOGETHER, THEN MULTIPLIED BY A THOUSAND--
--WELL, YOU'D STILL GET WHUPPED.
AND KORVAC'S NOT DISPLAYED THIS KIND OF POWER BEFORE...?
NO.

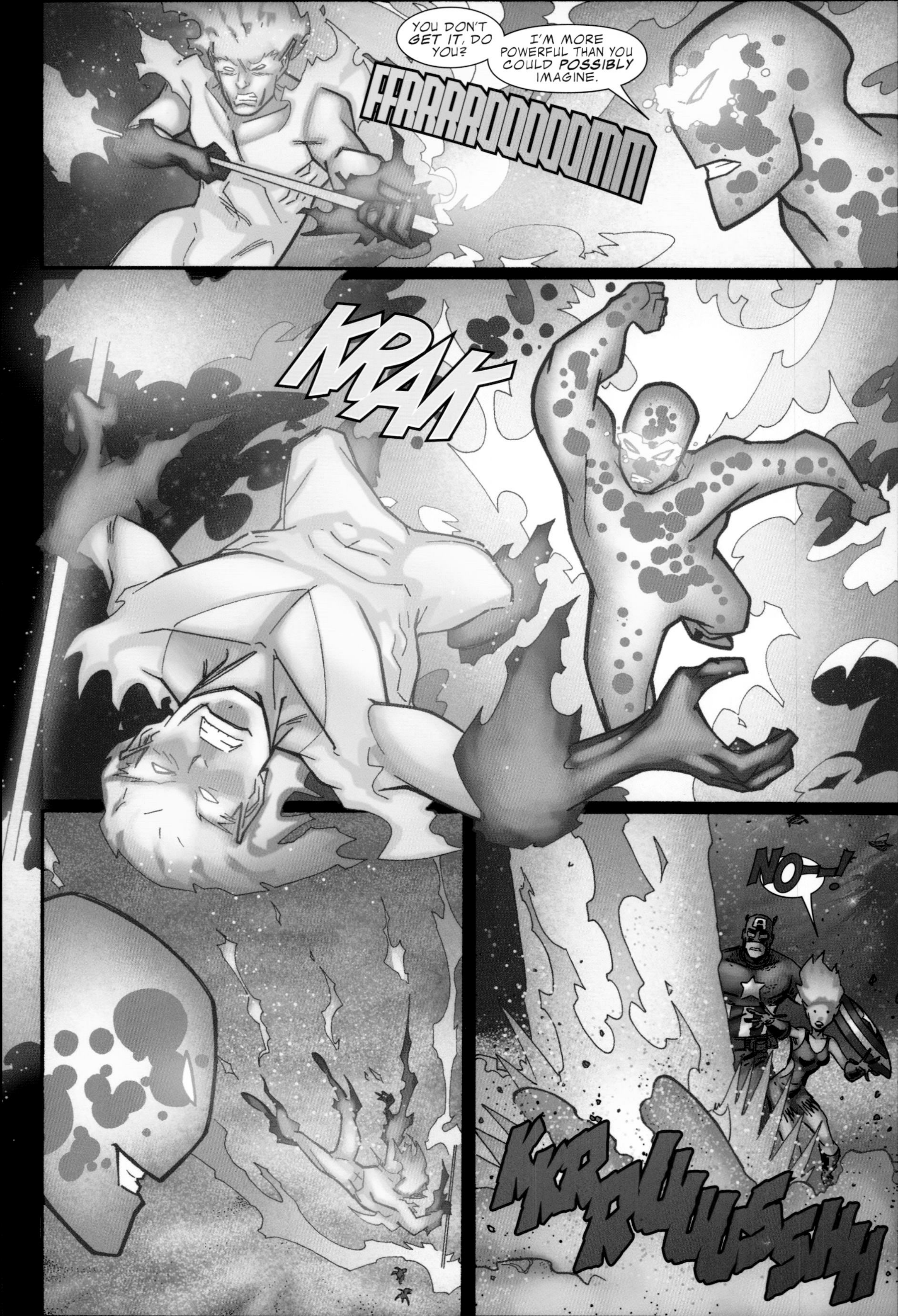

YOU DON'T GET IT, DO YOU?
I'M MORE POWERFUL THAN YOU COULD POSSIBLY IMAGINE.
FFRRRROOOOOMM
KRAK
NO--!
KKORRUUUSSHH

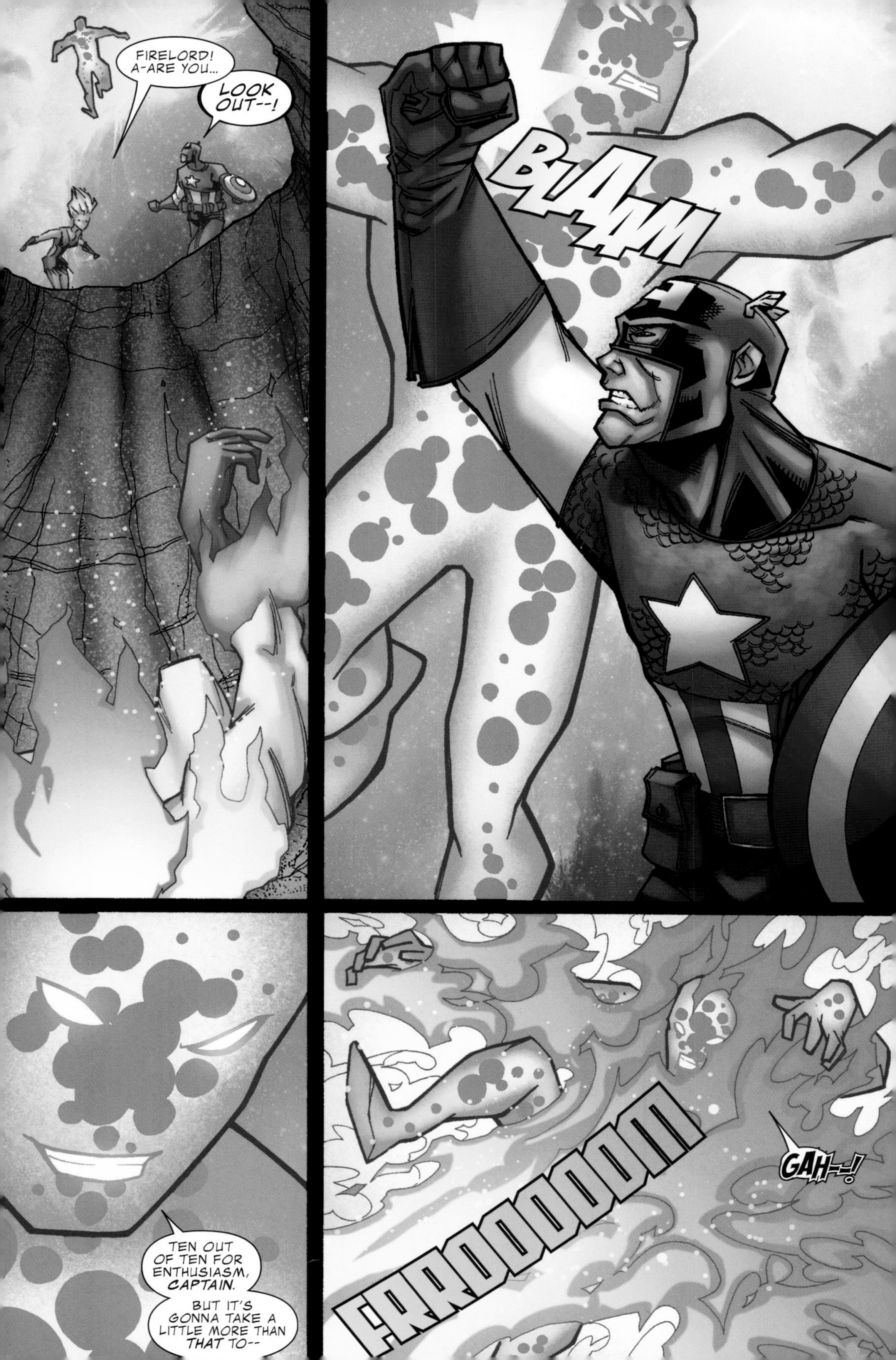
FIRELORD! A-ARE YOU...
LOOK OUT--!
BLAAM
TEN OUT OF TEN FOR ENTHUSIASM, CAPTAIN.
BUT IT'S GONNA TAKE A LITTLE MORE THAN THAT TO--
FRROOOOOOM
GAH--!

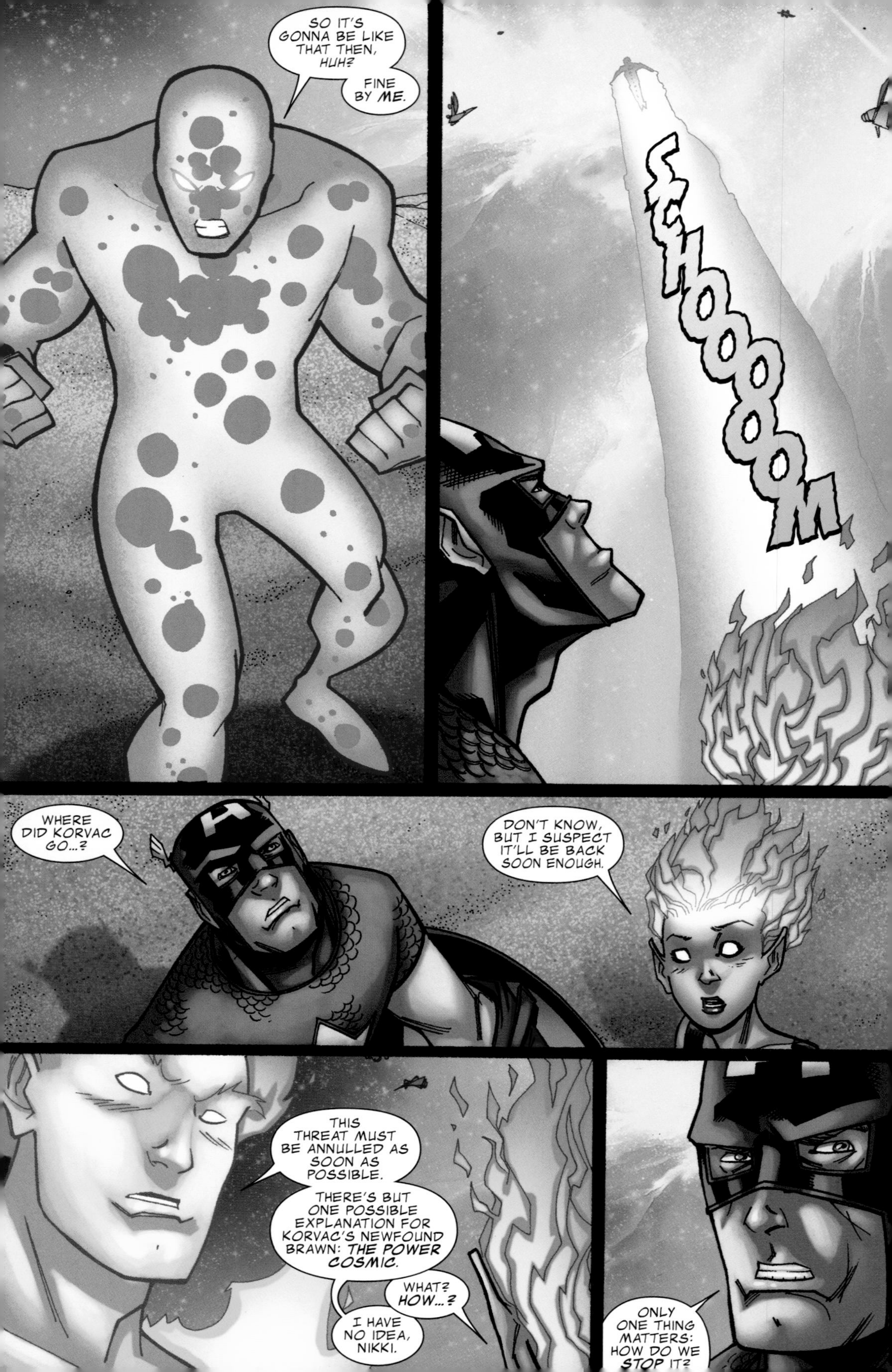
SO IT'S GONNA BE LIKE THAT THEN, HUH?
FINE BY ME.
SHHOOOOOM
WHERE DID KORVAC GO...?
DON'T KNOW, BUT I SUSPECT IT'LL BE BACK SOON ENOUGH.
THIS THREAT MUST BE ANNULLED AS SOON AS POSSIBLE.
THERE'S BUT ONE POSSIBLE EXPLANATION FOR KORVAC'S NEWFOUND BRAWN: THE POWER COSMIC.
WHAT? HOW...?
I HAVE NO IDEA, NIKKI.
ONLY ONE THING MATTERS: HOW DO WE STOP IT?

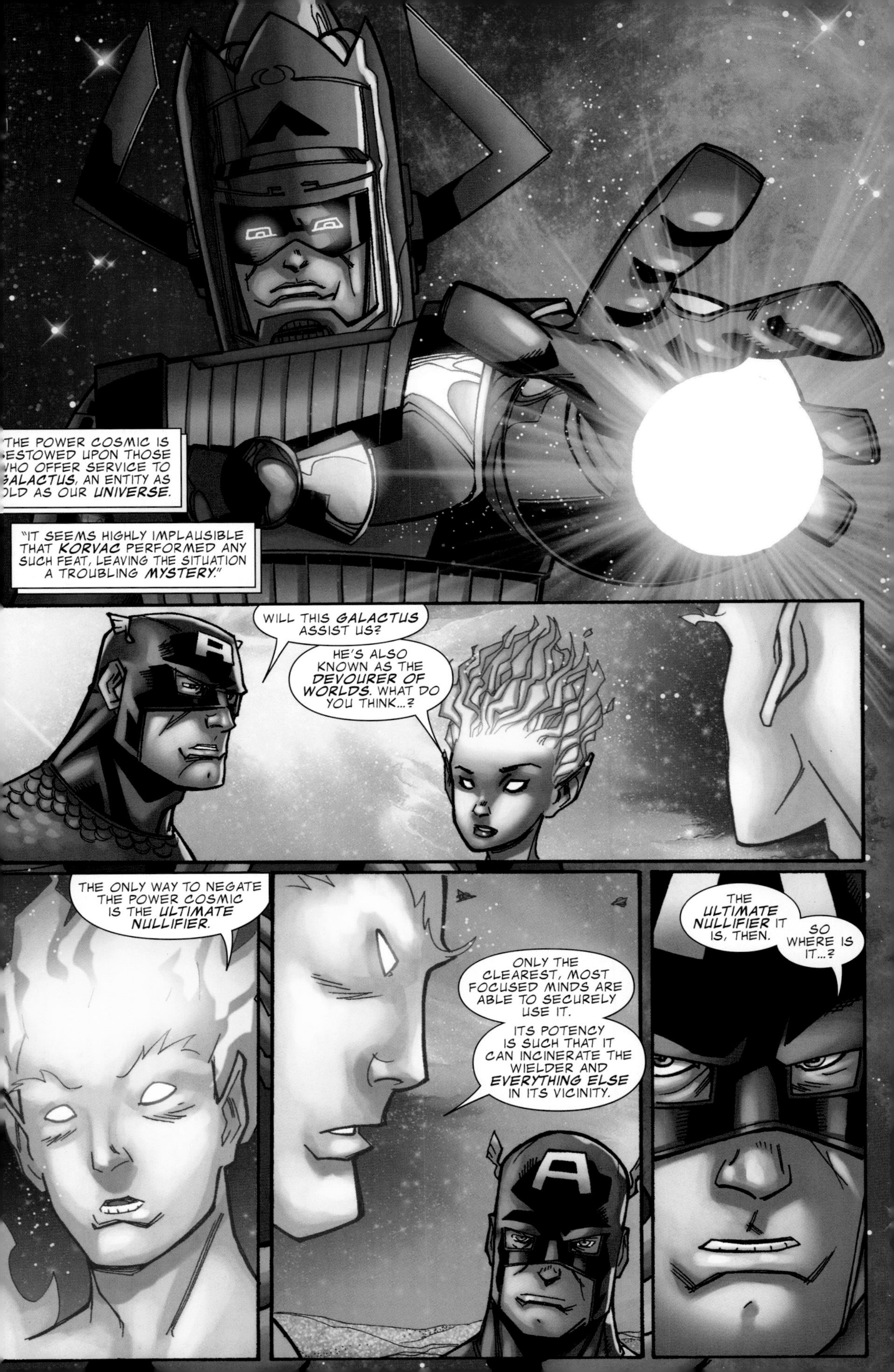

"THE POWER COSMIC IS BESTOWED UPON THOSE WHO OFFER SERVICE TO GALACTUS, AN ENTITY AS OLD AS OUR UNIVERSE.
"IT SEEMS HIGHLY IMPLAUSIBLE THAT KORVAC PERFORMED ANY SUCH FEAT, LEAVING THE SITUATION A TROUBLING MYSTERY."
WILL THIS GALACTUS ASSIST US?
HE'S ALSO KNOWN AS THE DEVOURER OF WORLDS. WHAT DO YOU THINK...?
THE ONLY WAY TO NEGATE THE POWER COSMIC IS THE ULTIMATE NULLIFIER.
ONLY THE CLEAREST, MOST FOCUSED MINDS ARE ABLE TO SECURELY USE IT.
ITS POTENCY IS SUCH THAT IT CAN INCINERATE THE WIELDER AND EVERYTHING ELSE IN ITS VICINITY.
THE ULTIMATE NULLIFIER IT IS, THEN.
SO WHERE IS IT...?

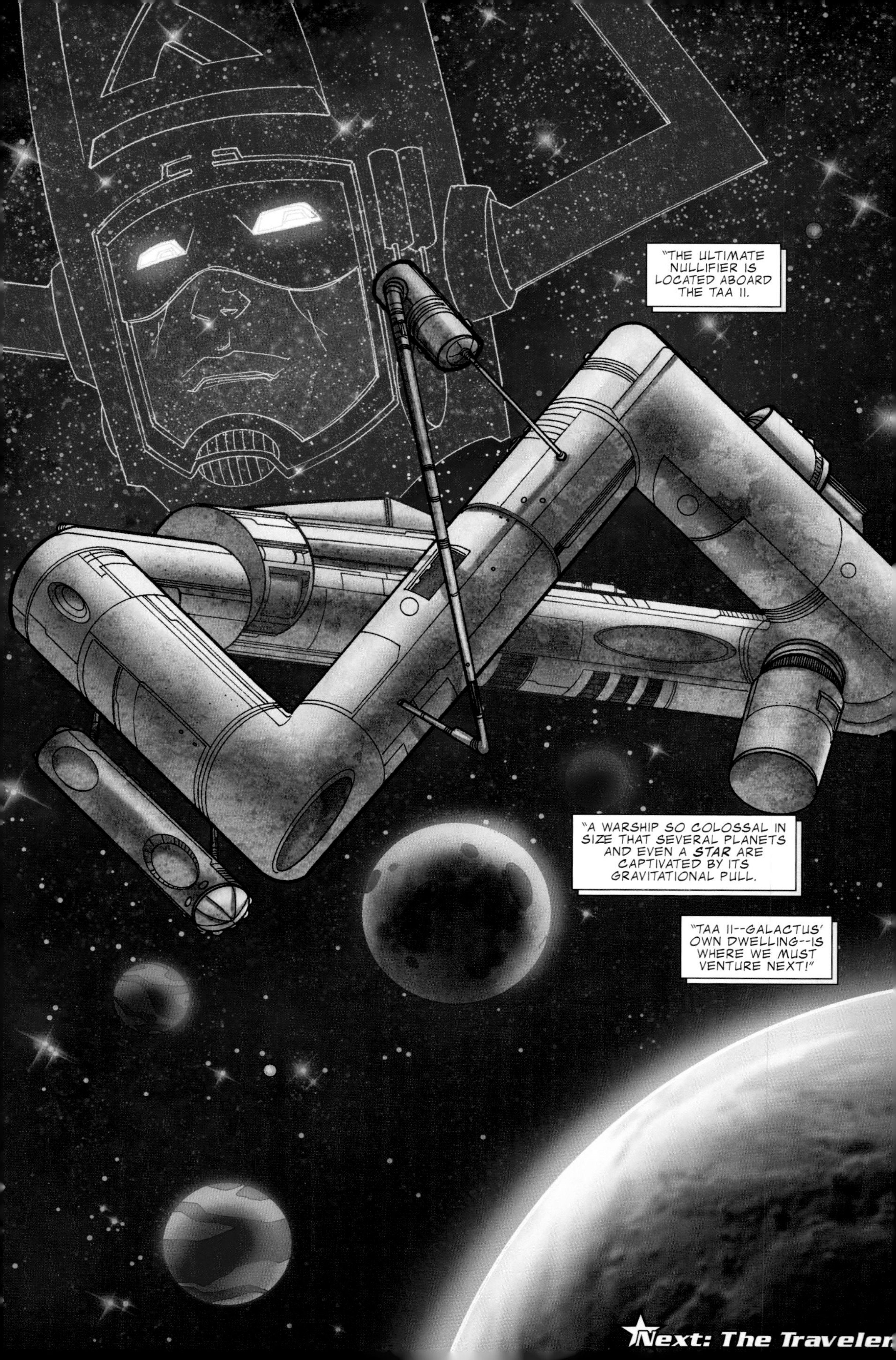
"THE ULTIMATE NULLIFIER IS LOCATED ABOARD THE TAA II.
"A WARSHIP SO COLOSSAL IN SIZE THAT SEVERAL PLANETS AND EVEN A STAR ARE CAPTIVATED BY ITS GRAVITATIONAL PULL.
"TAA II--GALACTUS' OWN DWELLING--IS WHERE WE MUST VENTURE NEXT!"
Next: The Traveler